NEW KiD

JERRY CRAFT

NEW KID

WITH COLOR BY
JIM CALLAHAN

HARPER
An Imprint of HarperCollinsPublishers

Library of Congress Control Number: 2018938256
ISBN 978-0-06-269119-4 (paperback) - ISBN 978-0-06-269120-0
(hardcover)

21 22   PC/LSCC   10 9 8 7 6 5
❖
First Edition

To the Jordan Banks in all of us

2

3

WHEW!

22

29

WELL, HERE I AM . . .

MY VERY FIRST CLASS . . .

AND I ALREADY CAN'T WAIT FOR THIS DAY . . .

. . . TO END!

RRRRRIIIIINNNNNGGGGGGGGGG!!!!!!!!!

YOU SURVIVED YOUR FIRST HOMEROOM.

WHAT CLASS DO YOU HAVE NOW?

UMMM . . . PRE-ALGEBRA WITH MR. GARNER.

ANDY SAYS I'M GONNA LIKE HIM.

CHAPTER 3

THE HUNGRY GAMES:
STOP MOCKING J

39

45

51

CHAPTER 4

UPPER, UPPER WEST SIDE STORY

Jordan's Tips for Taking the Bus

Fitting in on the ride to school is hard work!
I have to be like a chameleon.
For example, in Washington Heights,
I try to look tough.

Inwood is a little different, so I can lose the hood.
No one ever smiles in the morning, so you won't catch me doing that either!

Kingsbridge is where all of the public school kids get off, so it's okay to take off my shades. I can even draw!

Last comes Riverdale, where I do my best not to look cool AT ALL! No shades, and definitely no hood. I don't even like to draw 'cause PeoPle might think I'm GoinG to use my markers to "taG the bus"!

Man! By the time I Get to school, I'm exhausted!!!

58

Jordan's Guide to Fall Sports

First of all, our team name is *The Riverdale Academy Tadpoles*, or *The RAD Tads!* Ugh!

BRAD THE RAD TAD

This semester, everyone has to join a team or go out for the musical. I can't sing!

I thought about football, but then I thought about this!

JORDAN BANKS "IDIOT" BORN 20__ DIED VIOLENTLY

My other choices are cross-country, volleyball, competitive yoga, ultimate Frisbee (no joke), and soccer.

Even though I've never played before, Liam told me that all I needed to make one of our five soccer teams is a couple of these:

Team 1: Varsity

Team 2: Junior Varsity

Team 3: Thirds

Team 4: Lower Form A Team

Team 5: Lower Form B Team

Guess which one I made.

They even made me captain because I'm the only kid who NEVER threw up during practice AND has never had a concussion.

Now, the varsity games are amazing! Players soar high into the air to make acrobatic kicks!

And parents pack the stands to cheer for their kids.

YES! SCORE!!!

Meanwhile, *OUR* games look more like they're casting for a low-budget karate movie.

Parents use the time to check email or play *Words with Friends*.

YES! TRIPLE WORD SCORE!!!

Jordan Banks

80

WE DIDN'T EVEN COME **CLOSE** TO WINNING. IN FACT, WE LOST 11-1! BUT MY GOAL WAS THE FIRST ONE THAT A FIFTH'S TEAM HAD SCORED IN **SEVEN YEARS!** AND IT WAS THE **ONLY ONE** THAT WE WOULD SCORE ALL SEASON.

STILL, I ENDED UP LIKING SOCCER A LOT MORE THAN I THOUGHT. IT WAS NICE BEING ON A SCHOOL TEAM. WHO KNOWS—MAYBE I'LL EVEN GO OUT FOR A **SPRING SPORT** (EVEN THOUGH THEY'RE OPTIONAL). BUT HOPEFULLY ONE THAT PLAYS INDOORS . . . WITH **HEAT!**

CHAPTER 6

JORDAN BANKS:
THE NON-WINTER SOLDIER

CHAPTER 7

THE CHINESE FOOD CONNECTION

111

113

Taking Photos with My Mom
A Tale of Terror!

First, my mom can NEVER find her camera. It could be anywhere!

behind potato salad

Plus, it's really old! It used to be her dad's so she refuses to get a new one or use her phone. It still uses something called film! Google it!

Then she makes us take a *Jillion* shots in hopes that a few of them might *actually* turn out good.

But they almost never do!

127

Judging Kids by the Covers of Their Books!

MAINSTREAM BOOKS

AFRICAN AMERICAN BOOKS

MAINSTREAM BOOK COVERS:

Cool, colorful illustrations full of magic and hope!

MAINSTREAM BOOK PLOTS:

Prince Aimii leaves his dull life to slay a dragon, rescue Princess Brea, and prove to his father that one day he'll make a worthy king.

AFRICAN AMERICAN BOOK COVERS:

A depressing photograph full of realism and hopelessness.

AFRICAN AMERICAN BOOK PLOTS:

After moving to his third city in three years, DaQuell "Scooter" Jackson must decide if he will pursue his dream of being in the NBA or join a notorious gang.

MAINSTREAM BOOK HEROES:

* Lives in a magical kingdom!

* Lives in a stable home!

* Wants to live better!

* His father is king!

REVIEWS:

A thrilling magical tale
that is sure to inspire
readers of all ages to
never give up until they
have found the treasure
they seek.

–School Library Journal

AFRICAN AMERICAN
BOOK HEROES:

* Lives in the hood!

* Lives in a broken home!

* Just wants to live!

* His father is gone!

REVIEWS:

A gritty, urban reminder of
the grit of today's
urban grittiness.

–Jet magazine

Jordan Banks

138

CHAPTER 9

A KWANZAA STORY

149

151

BYE, MRS. LANDERS.

BYE, DEAR. COME BACK ANY TIME.

SO... ARE WE STILL COOL?

YEAH, WHY WOULDN'T WE BE?

AWESOME! MERRY CHRISTMAS, JORDAN! THIS IS FOR YOU.

WOW. THANKS!

BUT I DON'T HAVE ANYTHING FOR YOU.

YOU'RE MY FRIEND.

THAT'S A LOT!

POINT GAME, *LOSERS!*

C'MON, FELLAS, WE'RE PLAYING TERRIBLE!

ACTUALLY, YOU'RE PLAYING TERRI*BLY*.

173

175

CHAPTER 11

FIELD OF SCREAMS

The Baseball Hall of Shame!

When spring came we had the choice of baseball, crew, tennis, fencing, and some sport where you catch a ball with a net on a stick. That looked really hard.

I've never played any of those sports in real life, but at least I knew the rules from playing Major League Baseball 2K6 on Xbox. And watching games on TV.

my dad

For once, Drew didn't know how to play any of those sports either. Mainly because where he lives, there are even fewer parks than where I live.

Park!

The good news is that they put us on the same team. The bad news is that since so many kids went out for the *net-on-a-stick* game, they only had enough players for one lower-form baseball team. That meant Andy was on our team, too!

Jordan Banks

Then we found out why so few kids go out for baseball. His name is Coach Jim Bumdoody!

First of all, how can you not laugh at a name that has both "bum" and "doody" in it?

I'll tell you how: because rumor has it that some "hot dog" (that's what they call show-offs) made that mistake back in 1997.

And the coach ate him while his horrified team watched. I mean literally, too. Swallowed him whole!

That was one hot dog that didn't even need mustard.

192

193

A Public Service Announcement

AND AT THAT MOMENT, IT ALL BECAME *TOO MUCH!*

TOO MUCH OF KIDS LIKE ME TRYING TO FIT IN.

TOO MUCH OF KIDS WHO SHOULD FIT IN TRYING HARD NOT TO.

TOO MUCH OF GOOD KIDS BEING BLAMED FOR BEING BAD!

TOO MUCH OF BAD KIDS GETTING REWARDED FOR THEIR MEAN BEHAVIOR!

AND WAYYYY *TOO MUCH* OF ME FEELING LIKE I'M NEVER IN CONTROL OF *ANYTHING!*

CHAPTER 13
THE FARCE AWAKENS

▸▸ I TOSSED AND TURNED ALL NIGHT WORRYING ABOUT MY SKETCHBOOK.

Pork-fil-A
Double Bacon, Triple-Cheese Bacon Burger!

Sticks and Stones May Break My Bones But at LEAST Get My Name Right!

I used to think that when someone called me a name, that was the worst thing ever!

FATHEAD!

But you know what? I can deal with "Fathead" because my head isn't really fat.

my head

fat head

or names like "Stinky" because I don't stink. (For the most part!)

show-off!

I've even gotten used to Shorty, Oreo, Light (which is short for light-skinned), and a thousand other names that I've been called.

la
la
la
la

Because most times those names come from insecure people who want me to feel as bad about myself as they do about themselves.

221

CHAPTER 14

RAD MEN

245

249

To my family, Jay, Aren, and Autier.
Thank you for making me a better person.

Thanks to my agent, Judy Hansen,
my editor, Andrew Eliopulos, and Rosemary Brosnan
and the team at HarperCollins for embracing my vision.

Thanks to Marva Allen, Pam Allyn, Debra Lakow
Dorfman, David Saylor, Andrea Davis Pinkney,
and Andrea Colvin for inspiring me along the way.

Special thanks to my amazing colorist, Jim Callahan,
and to Jacqueline Woodson, Jeff Kinney, and Kwame Alexander
for your kind words and inspiration.

And last but not least, thanks to Barbara Slate,
Jim Keefe, Ray Billingsley, M'shindo Kuumba,
Eric Velasquez, Danni Ai, and Jennifer Crute
for making me a better artist.